You Can Make Magic!

in

Blackstone's Magic Adventures

Harry Blackstone, Jr., is one of the greatest magicians in the world today, and in his magic adventures, you help him solve crimes, help out people in trouble, and along the way, do some real magic tricks.

A whole world of excitement and fun awaits you in each new book. You decide which clues to follow; you decide which way to turn. You are the hero in the story!

If you take a turn that lands you in trouble, you can always go back and try again. And all through your adventure you'll find nifty magic tricks that will amaze your friends, and turn you into a real magician, too.

So what are you waiting for? The fun starts on page 5.

BLACKSTONE'S
MAGIC ADVENTURE ②

The Case of the Gentleman Ghost

MILO DENNISON

TOR

A TOM DOHERTY ASSOCIATES BOOK

BLACKSTONE'S MAGIC ADVENTURE #2: THE CASE OF THE GENTLEMAN GHOST

First printing: September 1985

A TOR Book

Published by Tom Doherty Associates
8-10 West 36 Street
New York, N.Y. 10018

Cover art by Fran Stiles
Interior illustrations by Paul Abrams

ISBN: 0-812-56253-4
CAN. ED.: 0-812-56254-2

Printed in the United States of America

It is the end of the summer season at Falcon Cliff Lodge, a fabulous mountain resort perched high above the swift-flowing Falcon River.

The lodge has been in business for over seventy years, always popular with celebrities. In the 1930s and 40s it was a favorite vacation spot for movie stars. In addition to sports and scenic views Falcon Cliff Lodge has a fully equipped theater, where many famous entertainers have performed for the guests.

This summer the main attraction is world-famous illusionist Harry Blackstone, Jr., who has been dazzling audiences with close-up magic and grand stage illusions.

Rita and Calvin are part of Blackstone's stage crew. They make sure the magical

Go to the next page.

equipment is in good working order, ready when Blackstone needs it—and safe from people who would like to know the magician's secrets. Both Cal and Rita practice their own tricks, and both of them want someday to have shows of their own.

Now the show is over for another evening. The theater is empty. Blackstone is in his dressing room, changing clothes. Cal and Rita are onstage, packing up equipment.

Suddenly, from just outside the theater doors, there is a woman's scream.

"What was that?" Rita says.

"Someone screaming," says Cal.

"I *know* that, silly. Maybe we should see what's happening."

Go to the next page.

"Sounds like a good idea. Should we call Blackstone first?"

The voice screams again.

Rita says, "I think we ought to get out there right now."

Do you want to go right now,
go to page 8.

If you call Blackstone from the dressing room,
go to page 12.

Without hesitating, Rita and Cal rush from the stage up the theater aisle and out the door.

They are in the lobby of the lodge, which has silver mirrors on the walls, a patterned wood floor, and an enormous crystal chandelier overhead.

Standing in the center of the lobby is a woman wearing a turban and a silk gown. She is still screaming, and the noise is starting to draw a crowd.

Rita says, "That's Countess Orsini, the perfume millionairess. She was at the show the other night."

Go to page 10.

"I remember," Cal says. "She wore that big diamond necklace."

Mr. Byron, the desk clerk, looks terribly worried. He puts his hands over his ears, then covers his round-rimmed glasses. "Please, Countess," he says, "not so *loud*." But no one seems to hear him.

The Countess stops screaming and starts to talk rapidly, gesturing wildly as she speaks. "And I come out of my bath, and there in the parlor he is standing, in white top hat and tails as for the fancy dress. On his face is a mask, white silk. In his hand

Go to the next page.

are my best diamonds. He tips his hat. He bows to me. Perhaps he would kiss my hand, but I do not let him do this. And he vanishes!"

"I'm going to get Blackstone," Rita says.

"Wait a minute," says Cal. "The thief might still be upstairs. He could get away."

If you go after the thief,
go to page 13.

If you want to find Blackstone,
go to page 12.

The two assistants rush backstage to Blackstone's dressing room door. Cal knocks, but there is no answer.

"Listen," Rita says, and they hear the sound of rushing water. "Blackstone's in the shower. We can't lose any more time."

Go to the next page.

Cal and Rita dash up the main staircase to Countess Orsini's suite. When they reach the third floor, Cal points down the hallway. "Look!"

There is a man standing there, in top hat and tails, all white, just as the Countess said. He has on a long white opera cape, lined with black. A cloth covers his face completely. He looks at Cal and Rita, takes off his hat to show snow-white hair,

Go to page 15.

and pours a bright stream of jewels from his gloved hand into the top hat.

Then he turns and runs around the corner, his cape billowing out behind him.

Cal and Rita run after him. When they get around the corner, they see the door to one of the hotel rooms standing open. At the end of the hall the window is open, and the curtain is fluttering.

If you check out the open doorway, go to page 16.

If you want to check the window, go to page 17.

Cal stops at the open door. Inside, a light is on by the bed, but no one is there. The heavy velvet curtains do not move: The window is closed.

"He just opened the door to slow us down," Cal says. "Let's check the window, quick."

Go to the next page.

Rita looks out the open window. There is no fire escape or any other way down: It is a sheer drop, three stories to the ground, and then down the cliffs to the Falcon Cliff itself.

If you want to take the stairs back down,
go to page 19.

If you call the elevator,
go to page 18.

The elevator arrives. On a stool in the corner of the car sits a man in a blue uniform: Charlie James, the elevator operator. A wooden cane is propped against the wall behind him. "Where to, friends?" he says.

Rita says, "The lobby, please."

"Next stop the lobby," Mr. James says, and pushes a metal grate across the door, then pulls a large brass control lever. The elevator starts going down.

Go to the next page.

When Cal and Rita get back to the lobby, a small crowd of people, guests and hotel staff, has gathered there under the crystal chandelier. "Really, now," Mr. Byron is saying, "I'm sure there's no need to worry." He doesn't seem to believe that himself, and no one is listening to him.

Go to the next page.

Rita says, "I think we'd better tell Blackstone."

"Tell me what?" says a voice behind her, and Harry Blackstone, Jr., walks into the lobby. Quickly Cal and Rita explain what they saw upstairs.

Blackstone nods. "And he just disappeared? This sounds serious." He looks up. "Hello, Ms. Christie. Have you got a ghost on the loose?"

Susan Christie, the hotel manager, is coming toward Blackstone, Cal, and Rita. She is a tall, blond woman, wearing a white suit with a rose in the lapel. "Have you ever known an old hotel that didn't have ghosts, Blackstone? Noisy pipes are ghosts, loose floorboards, flapping shutters—"

Go to page 22.

"The flapping shutter does not steal my diamonds!" Countess Orsini shouts.

"Calm down, ma'am," says a dark-haired woman in blue jeans and hiking boots. She is Kate Mackenzie, an engineer from a Denver mining company. She has on a vest with pockets for tools, and a flashlight and a hammer hang from her belt. "I just came up the road, and nobody went past me."

Blackstone says, "Is the road the only way in and out?"

"Yes," Ms. Christie replies. "Unless you have ropes and climbing gear. There's the path to the rock garden, but that doesn't go anywhere."

"Manager?" says a young man in a gray suit, with a gold watch-chain. His name is

Go to the next page.

Adam Randolph, and he is a lawyer for a movie company that wants to use Falcon Cliff Lodge as a setting for films. "Mr. Byron was just saying that this . . . jewel thief has appeared before."

Ms. Christie shakes her head. "Frank, you promised you wouldn't tell that story anymore!"

"It's my fault, I'm afraid," says a thin, mustachioed man in a red sweater, holding a cup of coffee. He shakes hands with Blackstone. "I'm Jack Shallow. I'm a writer. I asked Mr. Byron if he knew any, um, ghost stories . . . and he told me about Gentleman Jack. How could I resist a ghost with my name?"

"Have the police been called?" Blackstone asks.

Go to the next page.

Ms. Christie says, "Sheriff Morrison's on the way."

"Then, Mr. Shallow, maybe you should tell the rest of us about the ghost, until the sheriff gets here."

Countess Orsini shrieks, "And will the sheriff arrest the squeaking floorboard?"

Ms. Christie shakes her head again. "We'd all better stay in the lobby until Sheriff Morrison comes. I'll have the kitchen send some snacks up."

When everyone is settled with a sandwich and something to drink, Jack Shallow stands in front of the huge lobby fireplace and tells the story. . . .

Go to the next page.

"Forty years ago business was very good at the Falcon Cliff Lodge. The war had just ended, and people wanted to celebrate. The rules to save fuel were over, and they wanted to get in their cars and take long vacations. At resorts like this, they had a good time and dressed their best—and that meant wearing their best jewelry. Any night in the grand ballroom or the hotel theater you could see a hundred thousand dollars' worth of diamonds, emeralds, pearls—in today's money, maybe a million dollars' worth.

Go to the next page.

"Then one night the movie star Ada Milan woke up to find an uninvited guest in her room—a man in white evening clothes and a white silk mask, going through her jewelry box. Miss Milan screamed. The

Go to the next page.

man in white looked up, bowed to her, tipped his hat and dropped a pearl necklace into it, and walked out—through the open window!

Go to the next page.

"The rooms didn't have telephones then. Miss Milan kept yelling until a bellboy got there. He looked out the parlor window, but there was nothing there, no ladder or rope or ledge. Isn't that right, Mr. Byron?"

The desk clerk nods. "I was the bellboy who answered. There was nowhere he could have gone."

Mr. Shallow continues: "It went on like that for quite a while. The thief always bowed, or made some polite gesture; he never spoke, or threatened anyone. A couple of times the person being robbed said something like 'Please don't take that, it was my grandmother's'—and he always obeyed. And then vanished, just like magic. Excuse me, Mr. Blackstone."

"That's quite all right," Blackstone says.

Go to the next page.

"A magician is exactly what this jewel thief sounds like. Was he ever caught?"

"No. There were about a dozen robberies, and he was always seen. He never took more than one or two pieces, no matter how much jewelry was in the room, and he never took the most valuable items."

"Those are the hardest to sell, of course," lawyer Randolph says.

"That's true. But a funny thing happened. The rich guests started to *hope* the bandit—'Gentleman Jack,' they'd started to call him—would show up in their rooms. They knew he never hurt anyone, they all had lots of jewelry, and it gave them a thrilling story to tell. The police began to complain that the 'victims' weren't helping them, were even making things up to make their stories more exciting.

"And then, suddenly, Gentleman Jack disappeared for good. There were no more robberies, and none of the stolen jewels were ever found. There's a story that his loot is still hidden somewhere in Falcon

Go to the next page.

Cliff Lodge ... and that he'll come back for it someday."

"Looks like he has," Kate Mackenzie says.

The door opens and Sheriff Morrison comes in. He is a big man, dressed in a dark suit and a soft cap.

"He doesn't look much like a sheriff," Cal says to Rita.

"What were you expecting, cowboy boots and a six-shooter?"

"Hello, Mike," Susan Christie says to the sheriff, and explains what has happened.

Sheriff Morrison says, "Well, we sent the helicopter out to check the lodge road, but there was nothing. He could be hiding in the brush somewhere, but there's no point in looking until daylight."

Rita says to Cal, "Are you going to ask him if he has saddle blankets on his helicopter?"

"Okay, okay, sheriffs don't *have* to ride horses like in John Wayne movies."

The sheriff takes statements from everyone. When he talks to Blackstone, he says, "You must know something about making people disappear. Do you have any idea

Go to the next page.

where the, uh, ghost might have gone?"

Blackstone says, "I didn't see him, but my assistants did. Calvin? Rita? Do you have any ideas?"

The two think about what they saw upstairs.

If you stopped to check out the open door in the hallway, go to page 32.

If you went straight to the open window, go to page 33.

"We looked into a door he opened on the way," Cal says, "but there was no one there ... wait a minute! I think I know how Gentleman Jack disappeared!"

Do you know what Cal is thinking? You may check the description of the room on page 16 if you wish. When you think you know the answer, go to page 34.

"Gentleman Jack tricked us this time," Rita says. "He went into a guest room, and we went right past it. We thought he was trying to use misdirection, like a magician making you look at the wrong hand. But we outsmarted ourselves."

Cal says, "While we were looking out the window for him, Gentleman Jack just walked away. He could have gone anywhere."

Go to page 35.

"There were black curtains in the room, remember?" Cal says. "And Gentleman Jack had on a cape with a black lining."

"Of course," Rita says. "A Black Arts vanish!"

"Black magic?" Sheriff Morrison says, puzzled.

"No, no," Cal says. "If you put a piece of black velvet in front of a black background, it can't be seen from a distance. Magicians use velvet bags and curtains to make things appear and disappear on stage. We call it Black Arts."

Rita says, "Then, after we'd gone, Gentleman Jack just walked away."

Go to the next page.

"Well," the sheriff says, "we've got a very clever thief." He turns to the other people in the lobby. "Folks, I'd suggest that you all put your valuables in the hotel safe until we catch Gentleman Jack."

"Please, Mike," says the manager, "it's bad enough to have a thief on the loose, without his being a ghost from forty years ago, too."

The guests go upstairs to get their jewelry; Blackstone goes to his dressing room. Sheriff Morrison gets a sandwich and some coffee and sits down to talk with Ms. Christie, Cal, and Rita. A few minutes later the house telephone rings behind the front desk. Mr. Byron goes to answer it.

"Yes? I'm sorry, who is this? There's *what? Oh, my.*" He hurries around the desk. "Sheriff Morrison! Someone just called, and said there's a—there's a—"

"A what?"

Go to page 37.

Before the desk clerk can catch his breath to answer, there is an explosion from behind the desk. Papers flutter about, and a fire alarm starts to ring.

"—a bomb," Mr. Byron says.

The bomb has exploded inside an office near the front desk. Ms. Christie grabs a fire extinguisher and snuffs out the burning papers on the office floor. Then she looks around. "There wasn't much damage," she says. "Frank, what kind of voice was it on the phone?"

"Whoever it was, was disguising his voice—or hers, I couldn't tell. It was kind of . . . spooky." Mr. Byron laughs nervously. "And the call could have come from any room, since we got this fancy new electronic switchboard."

Ms. Christie laughs too. "And he or she made sure no one was hurt. So what was the bomb for?"

"Look at the safe, Susan," the Sheriff says.

The door of the safe has been blown off its hinges by the explosion. "Of course," the manager says. "Gentleman Jack doesn't want us locking up his loot."

Go to the next page.

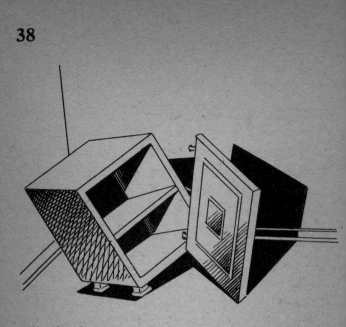

"Which proves he's no ghost," Cal says. "Why would he blow up the safe if he could walk through locked doors?"

Sheriff Morrison says, "I hope Gentleman Jack's out of tricks for one night. I'll bring a strongbox from the bank tomorrow, and the valuables can go in that. Good night, Susan. Good night, folks."

Calvin and Rita go up to their rooms. Cal says, "Do you suppose the ghost is one of the hotel guests?"

Go to the next page.

"Who else could it be?"

"Then who do you think it is?"

"I don't know yet," Rita says, "but if it's someone using magic tricks, then we've got to help catch him."

The next day all the conversation at the lodge is about the Gentleman Ghost.

"How polite he still is," Countess Orsini says over lunch, "warning you before his bomb goes off."

Writer Jack Shallow says, "I don't think he wants to hurt anyone."

"I'm glad you know what he's thinking," says Ms. Christie, the manager. "How about you, Mr. Blackstone? Can you tell what the ghost is going to do next?"

Blackstone, who has been talking to Cal and Rita about the mystery, turns and smiles. "Do you mean, can I read minds?" He reaches into his coat pocket and takes out a paperback book, and hands it to Ms. Christie. "This is one of Mr. Shallow's novels. It has three hundred eighty pages.

Go to the next page.

Would you pick a page number, please? And Mr. Shallow, please write the number down."

"Page one sixty-eight," Ms. Christie says, and Mr. Shallow writes it on a napkin.

Blackstone says, "There are about three hundred words on each page. Mr. Randolph, pick a word, please."

The lawyer thinks for a moment. "The one hundred thirtieth." Mr. Shallow writes it.

"Now," Blackstone says, "I'll go out of the room, and you look up the word you've chosen and write it down."

Blackstone leaves. Ms. Christie flips through the novel, and counts down the words on page 168. "The word is . . ." she says, and then stops and looks at Cal and Rita. "Wait a minute. You're his assistants. If you hear this, you might signal Blackstone."

"You're right," Rita says. "Just show Mr. Shallow the word, and have him write it."

Go to the next page.

They do so. After a moment Blackstone comes back into the dining room. "Do you have the word?"

"Yes."

"Would it be . . . 'ceiling'?"

"Yes, it would," Mr. Shallow says. "I wrote that book, and I couldn't memorize all the words."

Ms. Mackenzie says to Rita, "Did you give Blackstone a signal?"

"No, I didn't, and neither did Cal."

How do you think Blackstone did it? When you think you have the answer, go to page 42.

"Magicians don't usually give their secrets away," Blackstone says, "but I don't want you thinking I'm a ghost." He reaches into his coat again and takes out another copy of Mr. Shallow's book. "While you were looking up the word, I was looking it up too. Nobody expects a person to have two copies of the same book. I usually do the trick with a pocket dictionary, but I saw Mr. Shallow's novel in the gift shop and thought it would work even better."

"Thanks," Jack Shallow says, laughing.

Mr. Byron, the desk clerk, comes in. "Mr. Randolph, there's a letter for you at the desk. And Ms. Christie, the sheriff is here with the strongbox."

The group goes into the lobby, where Sheriff Morrison is waiting. Next to him is a large red metal box on wheels, bound with thick metal bands. It has a large brass

Go to the next page.

padlock. "This ought to hold all the important jewelry," the sheriff says. "If you folks want to bring your valuables downstairs, we can put them in now." He gives the box a push toward the office; one of the wheels squeaks loudly.

The guests go to their rooms and return with their jewel cases. Mr. Byron unlocks the strongbox and stacks the cases on the desk.

"Is that my letter?" Mr. Randolph says.

"Yes, sir," says Mr. Byron, and hands Mr. Randolph the envelope. The lawyer tears it open and shakes out a piece of paper. "Not much of a letter . . ." he says as he reads it. Then he gasps, and hands the letter to Sheriff Morrison.

Go to the next page.

The sheriff shows the paper to Blackstone. Cal and Rita read it too:

There's an old saying to beware of Greeks bearing gifts. I would add: Watch out for sheriffs bearing boxes—especially squeaky ones. You see, Mr. Blackstone, I have some tricks too.

Jack

Go to the next page.

"When did that letter arrive?" the sheriff asks.

"This morning," Mr. Byron says.

Mr. Randolph turns the envelope over. "It's postmarked from in town."

"There's a mailbox in the hotel," the manager says. "Anything posted there would get a town postmark and arrive the next day. Which still doesn't explain how that message got there."

"If you don't mind," Mr. Randolph says, "I've just got some cuff links and stuff. I think I'll keep them in my room."

"Starting to believe in ghosts?" Ms. Mackenzie says.

"I certainly believe in bombs," says the lawyer. "And you didn't bring any jewelry down at all."

The sheriff says, "Aren't you a mining engineer, Ms. Mackenzie?"

"Yes," she replies. "And yes, I know how to handle explosives. But I don't have any. I don't have any jewels, either. Just some

Go to the next page.

crystal specimens, part of my collection. You may check my room, if you wish."

"That isn't necessary," the sheriff says. "Mr. Blackstone, I'd like to talk to you, if I may."

Blackstone and the sheriff go out. The other guests leave, and the staff goes back to work. Cal and Rita are left in the lobby.

"Do you think the ghost will be back tonight?" Rita says.

"I'm sure he will," Cal says. "That note sounded like he was daring us to stop him."

"What are we going to do?"

"Watch for ghosts, of course. Blackstone doesn't have a show tonight, so we should get some sleep and watch later."

"But where?"

If you want to stay in the lobby tonight and watch the strongbox, go to page 47.

If you want to go ghost-hunting on the guest floors, go to page 58.

After dark Cal and Rita take up positions in the hotel lobby, well-hidden behind potted plants and furniture. The lights are dim except for a small lamp behind the front desk, where Mr. Byron is doing paperwork. The red strongbox is a few feet away from him.

Across the lobby the elevator door opens and Mr. James, the operator, gets out, leaning on his cane. "I'm going to the kitchen for some coffee, Frank," Mr. James says to the desk clerk. "No passengers this late. Want some?"

"Please, Charlie," Mr. Byron says.

After Mr. James has gone, the telephone rings, and Mr. Byron picks it up. He says something Cal and Rita can't hear. Then he hangs up the phone, and takes the strongbox key from a board where it hangs with dozens of other keys. He opens the strongbox and takes out one of Countess

Go to page 49.

Orsini's jewel cases, then puts the key back on the wall, where it is lost among the others.

He comes out from behind the desk and walks toward the stairs.

"What's he doing?" Cal says softly. "Could he be the ghost? Or the ghost's partner?"

"He could also be taking the jewels right into a trap," Rita says.

If you want to follow Mr. Byron,
go to page 50.

If you want to stay and watch the desk,
go to page 52.

Cal and Rita slip from their hiding place and follow Mr. Byron upstairs, being sure to stay out of sight. The desk clerk stops at Countess Orsini's floor, where Blackstone's assistants first saw the Gentleman Ghost. Mr. Byron goes to the Countess's door and knocks.

After several minutes the door is opened just a crack, and Countess Orsini's voice shrills, "What are you doing here at this terrible hour?"

"But, madam," Mr. Byron says, "you called and asked for your blue leather case."

"No such thing! Do I wear my pearls to bed, do you think? Go, now, go, or I shall see that you are fired!"

The door slams.

"It was a trick," Rita says. She and Cal race downstairs.

Go to the next page.

When they get to the lobby, a white top hat and a pair of gloves sit on the front desk. With them are a note:

> Very gentlemanly of you to make it so easy for me! Well, I have what I want, so I'll give you what you want: you won't be seeing the Ghost again.
>
> Jack

The strongbox is open, and all the jewels are gone.

"Fooled again," Rita says.

"Some detectives we are," says Cal.

This story ends here . . . but you can start over and try again.

A few minutes after Mr. Byron leaves, a figure dressed all in white steps into view from the side office. He reaches for the key that Mr. Byron replaced on the wall.

Cal yells, "Hold it, Gentleman Jack!"

The ghost turns. He is dressed in white evening clothes as he was before, but without the cape. Holding the key in one hand, he raises his cane and tips his hat with the other. Then the key vanishes from his fingers, and he runs around the desk, heels and cane clattering on the wooden floor. With Cal and Rita right behind him, Gentleman Jack races for the open elevator.

Jack makes it inside just ahead of the two detectives, and slams the door shut. The indicator arrow above the door shows that the elevator is rising.

If you want to race up the stairs,
  go to page 54.

If you would rather stay in the lobby and watch the strongbox, go to page 55.

Cal and Rita dash up the staircase to the third floor, where they nearly collide with Mr. Byron. The clerk holds the jewel case he took from the strongbox, and he looks worried. "What are you doing here?" he says.

Quickly the two explain.

"Oh, my," says Mr. Byron. "It wasn't really the countess on the phone, either. Where is the elevator going?"

They look at the indicator on this floor: The elevator is going back down. The three run downstairs.

When they get to the lobby, the elevator is open, and Mr. James is sitting inside, holding two cups of coffee. "I wondered who took the car upstairs," he says. "I'm sorry if I stranded you up there."

Breathlessly Cal and Rita explain what has happened.

"He's a lively old ghost," Mr. James says. "I hope you catch him."

Go to page 57.

The two detectives wait by the desk.
Finally Mr. Byron comes down the stairs,
still holding the jewel case, looking very
worried.

Ms. Christie comes into the lobby, dressed
in a robe and slippers. "Frank, what's
going on?" she says. "The Countess just
called me and demanded I fire you for
waking her up."

Go to the next page.

"It isn't his fault," Cal says, and explains about the ghost's appearance. Mr. Byron shakes his head. "I thought it was the countess on the phone, asking for this box," he says. "But it wasn't. Now I see why."

"It's a good thing you two were here," Ms. Christie says, "or the ghost could have grabbed all the jewels and vanished for good."

Mr. James appears, walking with his cane, holding two coffees in his other hand. "Well," he says, "I didn't know it was going to be a party, or I'd have brought more."

The manager laughs. "Some party, Charlie."

Go to the next page.

The next morning the sheriff arrives early and listens to the stories of what happened during the night. "So the key just disappeared out of his hand?"

"He probably used a sleeve vanish, like this one," Rita says. She shows the sheriff a piece of elastic cord, with a safety pin tied to one end and a cardboard tube on the other. Holding the tube with the thumb of one hand, she stretches the cord and holds the pin against her elbow. "You wear it pinned inside your sleeve, and stuff whatever you want to disappear into the tube. Then"—she lets go of the tube, and the elastic pulls it out of her palm—"zing! It's gone. That's one reason magicians say 'nothing up my sleeve,' and work with their sleeves rolled up: to prove they're not using one of these."

"Is there another key?" Mr. Shallow says.

"I've got one," says Ms. Christie, "but we'll have to keep an eye on the strongbox all the time now."

"No matter what anyone hears on the phone," says Adam Randolph.

Go to page 69.

Cal and Rita sleep for pat of the afternoon, getting ready for their nigh patrol. After dark they start walking up and down the dim hallways, looking for Gentleman Ghosts.

After a couple of hours this becomes very boring. "Maybe he's not going to show up," Cal says.

Rita says, softly, "Look!" Ahead of them Ms. Mackenzie's door is open.

Quickly and quietly they move to the door. One light is on. Gentleman Jack, dressed all in white, with his cane but without his cape, stands there: He is holding the crystal spheres from Ms. Mackenzie's collection. He smiles and points his cane at one more crystal ball.

It rolls along the stick into his hand.

Startled, Cal and Rita do nothing for a moment. And Gentleman Jack turns and steps through a glass door on the outside wall.

Go to the next page.

"There's a balcony outside this room," Rita says. "It connects to the bedroom window."

If you go into the bedroom,
   go to page 60.

If you go onto the balcony,
   go to page 62.

Cal tries the bedroom door, but it is locked. He knocks loudly. After a few minutes the lock clicks and Kate Mackenzie appears, in her nightgown. "What's going on?" she says.

Cal explains quickly, and Ms. Mackenzie rushes out onto the balcony. "I don't see him," she says. She looks at where her crystals were, and her voice is angry. "They weren't valuable to anyone but me," she says. "Some gentleman he is."

"We're sorry," Rita says.

"It's not your fault. You tried to stop him."

Cal and Rita leave. When they are nearly at their rooms, Cal says, "It is strange that he'd steal those crystals, if they're only worth a few dollars."

"Do you suppose he didn't steal them?" Rita says. "Could Kate Mackenzie be Gen-

Go to the next page.

tleman Jack? She could have waited for us to see her in disguise, then gone into the bedroom and changed quickly."

"Maybe," Cal says. "But it's too late to go back and search her room tonight, and by tomorrow everything will be hidden again."

The next morning, everyone hears about the gentleman's latest robbery.

"He must be getting desperate," Adam Randolph says. "Ms. Mackenzie says the stones are only worth a little: Why would Jack steal them?"

Go to page 65.

Rita rushes to the balcony. She looks down, but there is nothing there. She goes to the other door, but it is locked. The bedroom windows are dark.

Something whistles past Rita's ear and hits the balcony with a *crack*. She looks down: One of the crystal balls lies there, cracked now, sparkling with reflected light. Rita looks up and sees the end of a dark-colored rope disappearing past the edge of the roof.

Rita dashes back into the room. "Upstairs, quick!"

Suddenly the bedroom door opens, and Kate Mackenzie appears, in her nightgown, holding a steel hammer. "Hold it right there," she says. "What are you doing here?"

Rita explains as quickly as she can.

"I'm sorry I stopped you, then," Ms. Mackenzie says. "Go on, quick."

Rita and Cal race up the stairs to the roof, but there is no one there, only some

Go to page 64.

climbing stakes, pitons, driven into the roof, and a coil of nylon rope.

The next morning, Rita tells them about the rope and pitons. "That explains how he could walk right out an open window. The rope was waiting for him, and he went up it—but when anyone else looks out, the first thing they do is look down, giving him a few extra seconds to get away. A classic case of misdirection."

"Where could he have gotten the rope?" Mr. Randolph says.

"This is mountain-climbing country," says Ms. Christie. "Lots of stores sell rope and pitons. They're not likely to remember everyone they sold it to—and our ghost might have been in disguise."

"I just don't understand why he took my crystals," Kate Mackenzie says unhappily. "They were only valuable to me. It doesn't seem like a very gentlemanly thing to do."

Go to the next page.

"I think I can explain that," says Jack Shallow, walking into the room. The pockets of his red sweater are bulging. He takes out two handfuls of bright stones.

"My collection!" says Ms. Mackenzie. "You took them—"

"No, I didn't," Mr. Shallow says. "I thought I heard the maid come in while I was shaving this morning—but when I came out, the room hadn't been cleaned. So I looked around, and found these in my closet."

"Do you think Gentleman Jack tried to frame Mr. Shallow?" Rita says quietly to Cal.

"Either that, or Mr. Shallow is trying to keep us from suspecting him." Cal says aloud, "Could I have one of those for just a moment, please?"

"Certainly," Kate Mackenzie says.

Go to the next page.

Cal takes the ball, and pulls a piece of rope from his pocket. "Gentleman Jack did this with his cane," he says. "It's a bit trickier with a rope." And he rolls the ball back and forth along the cord.

How did Jack and Cal do this trick? When you think you know the answer,
go on to the next page.

Cal hands back the ball. Then he shows the rope, which has a piece of fine thread tied to each end. From only a short distance away, the thread cannot be seen. "Gentleman Jack must have had a thread like this, fixed to a couple of pins stuck into his cane. I just held the two strings a little way apart. Either way, they make a track for the ball to run along."

"That's a good trick," says Adam Randolph, "but it's not evidence in a crime. Who do you think Gentleman Jack is?"

"We're working on it," Cal says, as the breakfast dishes are taken away.

But as he and Rita leave the room, Rita says, "Mr. Randolph's right. We're not any closer to catching the thief."

And for the rest of the morning, the two of them work on cleaning and checking Blackstone's magical equipment . . . but they are thinking about Gentleman Jack.

Go to page 69.

Shortly after lunch a car pulls up to Falcon Cliff Lodge, and a man in an old-fashioned black suit gets out. The porter brings a large set of bags after him.

"Yes, sir?" Mr. Byron says.

"I am Eric Weiss," the man says. He has thick eyeglasses, a gray beard, and a heavy accent. "Weiss of Antwerp."

"Yes, sir. Would you like a room?"

"Of course I would like a room. This is a hotel, isn't it? I shall need a large room, with a good light, for my stones."

"Your what, sir?"

"*Stones*, young man. Have I not said, I am Weiss of Antwerp?" He takes one of the black bags from the porter and opens it. Inside, on velvet trays, are brilliant gemstones.

"Oh, my," Mr. Byron says, in a small voice. "Perhaps, sir, you would rather stay somewhere else. . . ."

"Why would I want to do that? This is where I want to stay. Do you not have a room?"

Mr. Byron says, "Well, sir . . . there's a jewel thief."

Go to the next page.

"Yes? I remember a jewel thief at this hotel. It is Gentleman Jack, you mean? Ha! Many years ago I was here when the gentleman was robbing the movie people. But Weiss he did not rob. And now he is back? Well, fine! Weiss of Antwerp is back too, and he invites Mr. Gentleman Jack to try again."

"Wow," Cal says, as the porter takes Mr. Weiss's bags upstairs.

Rita says, "Well, we know whose room to watch tonight."

Early in the evening Sheriff Morrison arrives back at the lodge. He does not mention Mr. Weiss or his jewels, but has dinner with Susan Christie.

After the meal the manager and the sheriff sit down with Jack Shallow and Kate Mackenzie to play bridge. As Mr. Shallow shuffles the cards, he turns to Blackstone and says, "Would you mind showing us another miracle?"

Blackstone stands up. "I have some things to do right now," he says, "but I'm

Go to the next page.

sure Calvin or Rita could provide a demonstration." Blackstone goes out.

"Would you mind?" the sheriff says. "We could let you get something ready."

"That isn't necessary," Rita says, and points at the deck Mr. Shallow is shuffling. "Pick a number from one to ten," she says, "and look at that card. Don't tell me what it is, but write it down."

Jack Shallow does so.

"All right," Rita says, "let me have the pack." She takes it and holds it behind her back. "Sheriff Morrison, would you give me a number higher than twelve?"

He thinks a moment. "Twenty-two."

Rita's hands work with the deck for a moment, and then she hands it back to Jack Shallow. "Now, count cards up to twenty-two, starting at the number you picked."

Go to the next page.

Mr. Shallow deals off cards. When he reaches twenty-two he turns the card up. It is the three of spades. He flips over the top sheet on the bridge score pad, and shows that he had written "3 of Spades."

"But I didn't tell you what the card was," the writer says. "I didn't even tell you what my number was."

Think about how Rita might have put the card at the right place. When you are ready, go on to the next page.

The trick depends on the person who chooses the card starting to count at his number, not at "one." When the sheriff chose twenty-two as his number, Rita counted off twenty-two cards, putting them in backward order, and then put them back on top of the deck. Then, when Mr. Shallow started counting from his chosen number, he had to reach the card he'd chosen.

Rita takes a bow, and the four bridge players go back to their game.

Rita and Calvin go back to their rooms, where they get flashlights for another Ghost Patrol. They go to the top floor, where Mr. Weiss's room is, and begin walking the halls.

Go to the next page.

Since it's late in the evening, the hall lights are dimmed. The electric lights, shaped like candles, throw long black shadows along the halls.

"Look," Cal says. "It's Mr. Weiss."

The gray-bearded jewel dealer leaves his room with a small, nervous look around. Cal and Rita hide in the shadow of a hall table; Mr. Weiss does not seem to see them. He goes down the stairs.

After a few minutes a cane pokes around the corner at the far end of the hall, followed by a white-trousered leg.

Gentleman Jack adjusts his top hat and strolls to Eric Weiss's door. He bends near the lock for a moment, then walks inside.

"You hold the door!" Rita says. "I'll get the sheriff!"

Calvin runs to the door and slams it shut, then leans his whole weight against it as Rita dashes downstairs.

In moments the elevator door opens, and Sheriff Morrison comes out, his gun drawn. Right behind him are Susan Christie and Rita. Charlie James, the elevator operator, leans out of the car, looking worried.

Go to page 76.

"He's still in here," Cal says, "unless he went out the window again."

"I've got a deputy outside, watching this window through binoculars," the sheriff says. "He didn't go that way. Okay, let me through."

Cal steps away from the door. "Police, Gentleman Jack," the sheriff says. "We're coming in!" He pulls the door open.

Inside stands a very surprised-looking man in a white tuxedo, his hands full with Eric Weiss's jewels.

"I don't believe it!" Ms. Christie says.

The man is Harry Blackstone, Jr.!

Go to the next page.

"I can explain," Blackstone says.

"You've got a lot of explaining to do," says the sheriff, "but you'd better call your lawyer first." He takes out his handcuffs.

"Wait!" Cal says. "Blackstone *can't* be Gentleman Jack. During the first robbery, he was in his dressing room."

"Did you see him there?" the sheriff says.

"Well . . . no," says Rita. "We heard the shower running."

"I'm afraid that's not good enough. Sorry, Blackstone, but you're under arrest." He snaps the handcuffs on Blackstone's wrists. "Don't you try escaping from those, either."

Blackstone says, "I'm sorry, Cal, Rita. I'll try to explain later."

When the group gets to the lobby, most of the guests are there to see the sheriff lead Blackstone out to a police car. They seem just as surprised as Cal and Rita.

"Well," Ms. Christie says as the car drives away, "at least the robberies are over and

Go to the next page.

we can all get a night's sleep." Everyone goes back to their rooms, leaving Cal and Rita all alone in the lobby.

"What are we going to do now?" Rita says.

"We've *got* to catch the real Gentleman Jack now," Cal says.

The next day everyone is talking about Blackstone's arrest. The guests are glad that Gentleman Jack is gone, but they all liked Blackstone and tell Cal and Rita how sorry they are.

Late in the morning porters bring Eric Weiss's bags downstairs, and Mr. Byron puts them behind the front desk.

"Where's Mr. Weiss?" Cal asks.

"He was called away suddenly," Mr. Byron says, "and will send for his bags tomorrow. Until then, we'll keep them here. Thank goodness all this Ghost business is over." He pauses and scratches his head.

Go to the next page.

"Of course, I said that forty years ago. Oh, my."

Cal and Rita agree that the real Gentleman Jack is surely going to try and steal Eric Weiss's jewels tonight.

"When that happens," Cal says, "at least the sheriff will know that Blackstone is innocent."

"But that doesn't save Mr. Weiss's gems," Rita says. "We have to set a trap for Jack— one he won't get out of this time."

Rita and Calvin crouch in the darkened hotel lobby, where they have a clear view of the front desk, the elevator, and the stairs.

The elevator door slides open and Mr. James comes out, his cane tapping. "Good evening, Frank," he says to Mr. Byron. "Do you want some coffee?"

"That's just what he said when the strongbox keys were stolen," Rita says. "Do you suppose Mr. James could be Gentleman Jack?"

Go to the next page.

"But Mr. James has a limp, and Jack can run up stairs and climb ropes."

"He could be faking the limp."

"That's true," Cal says.

Charlie James says, "I'll be back from the kitchen in a moment, Frank."

*If you want to follow Mr. James,
go to page 81.*

*If you'd rather stay in the lobby and watch,
go to page 97.*

Moving very quietly, Cal and Rita leave their hiding place in the lobby and follow Charlie James toward the kitchen. He goes through the kitchen door, which swings shut behind him.

"I guess he's really getting coffee," Cal says.

"Maybe not," says Rita. "There must be more doors than this one."

If you want to go on into the kitchen,
go to page 82.

If you go back to the lobby,
go to page 102.

Rita pushes open the kitchen door. Mr. James is leaning against a table, holding a cup of coffee and talking to the cook. "Hello there," he says. "Are you two hungry?"

Go to the next page.

"We were—" Rita says, "that is, we thought—"

"We'd better get back to the lobby, quick," Cal says.

Go to the next page.

They race back to the front desk. When they get there, Mr. Byron is sitting quietly, reading a book. "Is anything wrong?" he asks.

Cal says quickly, "Are Mr. Weiss's bags all right?"

"Why, yes. They're right here."

Mr. James appears. He hands a cup of coffee to Mr. Byron. He looks at Calvin and Rita. "Why were you two in the kitchen?"

Rita says slowly, "We, uh, thought you were Gentleman Jack."

"Oh," Charlie James says, and smiles sadly. "Well, you're right. I was. Let's go back to the kitchen and talk about it over a piece of pie."

Go to the next page.

Sitting in the kitchen, Charlie James tells this story:

"Forty years ago I wanted to be a dancer in the movies, like Fred Astaire or Bill Robinson. I got a job with Silverchrome Studios, for a few dollars a week. I wanted to be a star, but I was just an extra, I never had any lines, and there didn't seem to be any way of making the movie company notice me."

"Then Silverchrome made a movie called *The Society Bandit*, about a jewel thief. I played a cabdriver in it, and it gave me an idea of how to get myself noticed. The company came out here to Falcon River to make some westerns, and all the important people stayed here at the lodge. The rest of us lived in a camp in the hills, not far away.

Go to the next page.

"At night I'd take a white tuxedo from the costume wagon and sneak into the lodge. I'd make sure somebody saw me—and I never threatened or hurt anybody. I wasn't even going to keep the jewels. When everybody had heard about Gentleman Jack, I was going to appear and give everything back."

Mr. Byron shakes his head. "I've been wondering for forty years, Charlie, now I've got to ask. How did you disappear out of Ada Milan's window?"

Mr. James smiles. "I had a rope tied to the gutter brackets on the edge of the roof. When somebody looks out of a window, they almost always look *down* first. That gave me the few seconds I needed to climb up and disappear onto the roof."

"More misdirection," Cal says.

Mr. James nods, and sighs. "But I got to like playing Gentleman Jack too much, and I pushed my luck too far. Thieves always

Go to page 88.

do, I guess. One night I stepped out to grab my rope—and I hadn't tied it properly. I fell, and broke my leg very badly. I never went back to the movie company's camp."

"Didn't anyone miss you?" Rita says.

"The movies then weren't like they are now. There weren't a lot of laws to protect us, and if you got hurt, and weren't a big star, they just wanted you to go away and not make trouble. Besides, I was afraid that if I tried to explain how I'd broken my leg, they'd guess that I was the jewel thief."

Cal says, "What happened to the jewels?"

"I sold the ones I had with me to pay a doctor for treating my leg—and not telling anyone. I'd hidden most of the loot out in the hills, high up." He touches his cane, and rubs his bad leg. "I couldn't hike up there to get them, and after all these years I don't have any idea where they are.

"Since I couldn't dance anymore, I didn't

Go to the next page.

want to be in the movies anymore either. And Falcon Cliff Lodge had a job for an elevator man—just the thing for me, since I could do it without walking too much. And here I've been, for all those years, hearing the legend of Gentleman Jack."

"You fooled me long enough," Mr. Byron says.

"You aren't angry, are you, Frank?"

"Of course not, Charlie."

Rita says, "But this doesn't help us find the new Gentleman Jack. We know Mr. James can't be guilty—this thief runs too fast."

"We need to set a trap," Cal says. "Jack thinks he has all the valuable gems at the Lodge. But what if we found the original Gentleman Jack's loot?"

"But I told you," says Mr. James. "I don't know where it is."

Cal says, "But the ghost doesn't have to know that."

Go to the next page.

The following morning Mr. James tells the story of the original Gentleman Jack to all the guests—all except the part about forgetting where the loot was hidden.

"Rita and I went out this morning and got the jewels," Cal says. "We'll have to figure out some way of getting them back to the owners or their families."

"Where are the gems now?" Kate Mackenzie asks.

Rita says, "Magicians are good at hiding things. We've put them inside some of Blackstone's equipment."

Countess Orsini says, "Where the rest of his stolen jewelry is hidden, no doubt."

"Blackstone didn't steal anything," Cal says, "and we'll prove it."

"My jewels he certainly did not steal," says Mr. Weiss suddenly from the corner of the room. No one saw him come in.

Go to the next page.

"And he will not now. I will take my bags now, please."

Mr. Weiss leaves with his suitcases. "That's better for our plan," Cal says. "Now Gentleman Jack has to come after the jewels we said we have."

For Cal and Rita the day goes by slowly, as they wait for the night and the appearance of Gentleman Jack. They work backstage, making special preparations.

That evening, Cal and Rita say good night early to the other guests.

"Aren't you worried about the old gentleman's jewels?" Kate Mackenzie says.

Rita pretends to be very sleepy and not very interested. "Not really," she says. "You'd have to saw somebody in half to get at them."

Blackstone's assistants go up to their rooms, then, a few minutes later, slip back

Go to the next page.

downstairs to the theater and hide near the lighting control panel. Out onstage are a few crates and a long table.

They wait for an hour, two hours, three. "Maybe Gentleman Jack didn't understand our clue," Rita says.

"Look!" says Calvin.

The jewel thief, dressed in his fancy white suit, strolls up the theater aisle, twirling his cane. He walks straight up to the long table, bends over it, and knocks on it with the head of his cane. Then he reaches along the edge of the table.

The top of the thin table swings up. Gentleman Jack stops still.

"Now!" Rita says, and Cal switches on the stage spotlights. Gentleman Jack is flooded with light. He turns to run off-stage, but sees someone standing right in his path. He runs in the other direction—

Go to the next page.

straight into Cal and Rita, who pin him down to the floor.

Suddenly the theater doors open, and Eric Weiss, the gem dealer, comes in, followed by Sheriff Morrison and two deputies.

"Bravo!" Mr. Weiss says. "Well done!" He does not have his Dutch accent any longer, and his voice is very familiar.

"Blackstone!" Cal and Rita say at once.

Mr. Weiss pulls off his false hair and beard, and indeed he is Harry Blackstone, Jr. "Now," Blackstone says, "let's unmask our gentleman friend."

Rita takes hold of the white silk that completely covers Gentleman Jack's face, and pulls it away.

It is Adam Randolph, the lawyer.

After the sheriff's deputies take Gentle-

Go to the next page.

man Jack away, everyone gathers in the theater to congratulate the two detectives. "I'm sorry we tricked you," Blackstone says, "but we had to make the real thief think that the police weren't watching."

"We understand," Cal says. "And we should have guessed it was a trick, by the name you chose for your disguise. We should have remembered who Ehrich Weiss was."

"But who was he?" Ms. Christie asks.

"He changed his name when he became a magician," Rita explains. "To Harry Houdini!"

Sheriff Morrison asks, "How did you get Mr. Randolph to look at the table first thing?"

"We knew he knew some magic, so we gave him a hint," Rita says. "I said you'd have to saw someone in half to find the jewels." She goes to the table and lifts its top, showing a surprisingly deep space in-

Go to the next page.

side. "This is the kind of table magicians used to use to do the sawing-a-person-in-half trick. It's made to look thinner than it really is. The person who's being 'sawed' has lots of room to drop down inside it and let the saw go by." She reaches into the table, takes out a large sign, and holds it up. FOOLED YOU, it says.

Jack Shallow asks, "How did he send that message to himself, about the strongbox?"

"He mailed himself an empty envelope," Cal says, "that had a little slit cut in its flap. He didn't know what message he would put in, only that it would be something to draw suspicion away from himself. The strongbox was perfect, and very mysterious. He wrote the note, and then when he got the envelope from Mr. Byron, he slipped it through the slit. When he tore the envelope open, all the evidence disappeared."

"One more question," Kate Mackenzie

Go to the next page.

says, pointing at the backstage EXIT sign. "The sign points that way out. Why did he run in the other direction?"

"He saw a ghost," says a voice from offstage. Charlie James comes in, dressed in a white Gentleman Jack tuxedo. Leaning on his cane, he does a little soft-shoe dance step, and tips his top hat.

Mr. James turns the hat over, and a stream of jewels—Adam Randolph's loot—pours out into Cal and Rita's hands.

The audience applauds.

THE END

After Mr. James leaves, Mr. Byron goes back to his books.

Suddenly a person dressed all in white steps silently from the side office to stand behind Mr. Byron. Gentleman Jack raises his cane and hits Mr. Byron over the head. He groans and falls to the floor. Then Jack bends over Eric Weiss's gem cases.

"Quick!" Cal whispers, and he and Rita run to the desk, each blocking one end of it. Gentleman Jack looks from one of them to the other. Then he leans on his cane and jumps over the desktop, a bag of jewels still under his arm. He turns to run.

Charlie James comes around the corner, cane in one hand, coffee in the other.

"Stop him!" Rita yells.

The ghostly thief takes a quick step. Mr. James moves faster. He puts out his cane and trips Gentleman Jack, who goes skidding across the floor. Mr. Weiss's gems scatter everywhere. Cal and Rita race around the desk and pin the thief down.

"Frank, call the sheriff," Mr. James says. "Well, now, will you look at this?" He

Go to page 99.

points to where one of the jewels hit the floor. It has broken into a thousand pieces.

"Jewels don't break," Cal says. "It was glass."

"And it won't be necessary to call me," says Sheriff Morrison, from the doorway. With him is Mr. Weiss.

Rita says, "Mr. Weiss, your jewels—"

"Are fakes," says the gem dealer, "just like me." And he pulls off his gray hair, glasses, and beard—to show the face of Harry Blackstone, Jr.!

"Now, let's see who's behind the other disguise," the sheriff says.

"All right," says a voice, muffled by the silk that covers Gentleman Jack's whole face. The gloved hands come up and pull the mask away.

"*Susan?*" says Sheriff Morrison.

"I'm sorry, Mike," says Susan Christie, the Gentleman Ghost.

"I did it for the hotel," the manager says. "I thought that if the story about the return of Gentleman Jack got to be news, people would come here out of curiosity. I

Go to the next page.

wasn't going to keep all of the jewelry—when business was good again, it would have been found, hidden."

"I think I can guarantee you some publicity," Jack Shallow says. "I'm definitely going to write a book about the Gentlemen Thieves."

"But you broke the law, Susan," the sheriff says unhappily. "I'm going to have to arrest you."

Ms. Christie nods.

"Well, you're going to need a lawyer, and I guess you've got one," Adam Randolph says. "How did you send that letter to me, about the strongbox?"

"We've had trouble with the safe before," Ms. Christie says, "and I remember that old strongbox very well. When I decided to wreck the safe, I just mailed the letter to one of you at random." She turns to Mr. Byron, who has an icebag on his head. "I'm sorry, Frank, but I couldn't think of anything that would get you away from this desk, not after the other times.

Go to the next page.

You're very loyal . . . and I think you ought to be the new manager."

"Oh, my," Mr. Byron says.

"And the jewels?" Blackstone says.

Susan Christie hands her cane to Rita. "Put this on that little brass plate, there by the front desk, and turn."

Rita does so. There is a small click as the brass tip of the cane turns the plate. Then the front panel of the desk slides open, and light shines on a rainbow cascade of jewels.

Rita hands the cane back. "Keep it," Ms. Christie says, and hands her top hat to Calvin. "Souvenirs, for Blackstone's ghost-breakers, from the Gentleman Ghost."

She takes a small bow as the sheriff leads her away. And almost in spite of themselves, the audience applauds.

THE END

When Cal and Rita get back to the lobby, Mr. Byron is lying on the floor. He groans and rubs his head.

"What happened?" Rita says, and helps Mr. Byron sit up.

Go to the next page.

"Someone hit me over the head," he says, and looks around. "Oh, my . . . Mr. Weiss's bags are gone."

Mr. James appears. He hands a cup of

Go to the next page.

coffee to Mr. Byron. "Jack gets to be less of a gentleman all the time," he says.

"At least this proves Blackstone is not the thief," Rita says. "We have to call the sheriff and tell him."

"I'll do it," Mr. Byron says. He makes the phone call. "The sheriff says he'll be here right away."

"That might not be quick enough," Cal says. "We can't give Gentleman Jack time to hide the jewels. We have to go after him now."

Go to the next page.

Think about what Cal and Rita have seen. When you think you know the answer, go to the page for the person you think is guilty.

Who do you think Gentleman Jack is?

Countess Orsini?
  Go to page 106.

Jack Shallow, the writer?
  Go to page 114.

Kate Mackenzie, the engineer?
  Go to page 110.

Adam Randolph, the lawyer?
  Go to page 109.

Cal and Rita knock on Countess Orsini's door. When the door is opened, they rush inside.

Go to the next page.

"What is all this about?" says the countess. Mr. Weiss's bags are not there.

"We thought . . ." Cal starts to say. "Uh . . . I guess we were wrong."

Go to the next page.

"You think I am the thief?" the countess says angrily. "How can I be this gentleman, when I am the first one he robs?"

"That's right," Rita says. "We saw Gentleman Jack upstairs while the countess was down in the lobby."

"Some detectives we were," Cal says. "Now we may never find Mr. Weiss's jewels."

Go to page 111.

Using a key borrowed from Mr. Byron, Blackstone's assistants burst into Mr. Randolph's room. It is quite dark inside. Mr. Randolph turns on a light and sits up in bed. "I didn't order room sevice," he says. Mr. Weiss's suitcases are nowhere in sight.

"I think we made a mistake," Rita says. "We're sorry."

"Don't worry," Adam Randolph says, smiling. "I won't sue you."

Go to page 111.

When the two detectives knock on her door, Kate Mackenzie answers right away. She opens the door just a crack and says, "Isn't it kind of late for a visit?"

If you change your mind and leave,
  go to page 111.

If you insist on going inside,
  go to page 112.

Rita and Calvin go back to their rooms. They know that the sheriff will be here soon, and Blackstone will be free—but no one may ever catch the Gentleman Ghost.

This story ends here. But you can start over and try again.

"Well, all right, come in," Ms. Mackenzie says. "I don't know what you're looking for, though."

Rita and Cal look around the room. They see nothing but some rock specimens and tools.

Suddenly there is a loud thump on the door to the hallway. "*More* visitors?" Kate Mackenzie says tiredly, and opens the door again.

A silver letter opener, shaped like a dagger, is stuck into the door. Hanging on it is a note, on the Lodge's letter paper. The message reads:

> My compliments to the two young detectives for being so hot on my trail. Ghosts should never be greedy, so I think I'll vanish before I'm caught. See you again in forty years.
>
> Gentleman Jack.

Go to the next page.

"He's gone," Cal says. "Now we'll never find him."

This story ends here. But you can start over and try again.

Cal and Rita rush to Mr. Shallow's room. He answers the door dressed in his pajamas and robe. He seems very sleepy. "Yes?" he says, and yawns. "What can I do for you?"

If you change your mind and leave,
   go to page 111.

If you go on into the room,
   go to page 115.

Cal says, "We'd like to take a look around if we may."

"Sure," says Mr. Shallow. He opens the door. Inside there is nothing suspicious, only some books and papers.

One of the papers is a photocopy of an old newspaper. Its headline reads GENTLE-MAN BURGLAR STRIKES AGAIN!

There is a thump at the window. "What's that?" Rita says.

"Time to go!" Jack Shallow shouts, and runs for the door to the balcony outside his room. He slams the door behind him, almost breaking the glass. Cal and Rita dash after him.

When they get out on the balcony, there is no one there.

If you have ever been on one of these balconies before, go to page 116.

If not, go to page 118.

Rita remembers that the last time she chased Gentleman Jack onto a balcony, she saw nothing down or to the sides. *So,* she thinks, *he must have gone up!* She looks up, just in time to see the end of a rope wriggling over the edge of the roof. "Call Sheriff Morrison," she shouts. "Tell him to send his helicopter!"

The sheriff answers the radiotelephone in his car, and orders the stairs from the roof to be locked. In a few minutes, the police helicopter is whirring overhead, shining a brilliant light onto the Lodge roof.

"All right!" shouts Jack Shallow, also known as Gentleman Jack. "I'll come down!"

Cal and Rita watch the helicopter from the balcony. It turns, and they see Harry Blackstone, Jr., waving from its window.

Go to page 119.

Cal and Rita hurry downstairs. "Call the sheriff!" Cal tells Mr. Byron.

The sheriff answers the radiotelephone in his car. "So it's Jack Shallow we're looking for? I'll get patrols out at once. He won't disappear this time." After a moment, Sheriff Morrison says, "Someone else wants to talk to you."

Blackstone's voice comes over the telephone. "Nice detective work, you two. Thanks for helping me get out of that jail. It was a pretty neat escape."

This story ends here. But if you'd like to try again, and perhaps solve some other mysteries, you can start over.

After the sheriff has taken Gentleman Jack Shallow away, Cal and Rita show everyone the papers they found in his room.

"Mr. Shallow was doing research to write a book," Rita says, "and learned about Gentleman Jack. He had written mystery novels before, but this time he decided to make a mystery of his own."

Adam Randolph says, "But how did he send me the letter about the strongbox?"

"He didn't send it to you, at first," Cal says. "He mailed an empty envelope to himself, sealed with rubber cement, with his address written on a stick-on label. He got the letter the next day, peeled off the label, and wrote your name and address on the envelope. Since the flap was just

Go to the next page.

stuck shut with rubber cement, it opened easily. Then he wrote his mysterious message, sealed the envelope again, and dropped it into the pile of mail before Mr. Byron could sort it."

"But how did he know about the squeaky strongbox?" Kate Mackenzie asks.

"He didn't, exactly," Rita says. "When he sent the envelope he just knew he was going to make up a message to fool us all. Then he knew that a strongbox was coming, because the sheriff said so. You remember, the message just said 'squeaky old box,' not 'squeaky-wheeled box.' It was easy and safe to guess that *something* on the box would squeak, and we'd all remember it as being a much more accurate prediction. That's how a lot of 'psychic' magic tricks work."

Go to the next page.

"You've been learning very well," Blackstone says. "Thanks for helping me 'escape' from jail."

"But my diamonds?" Countess Orsini says. "Are they all disappeared still?"

"For our next trick . . ." Rita says, and Cal puts Jack Shallow's books on the table. He opens the cover of a thick dictionary, turns back a few pages—and shows that the book is hollow inside. Gemstones blaze like multicolored fire.

The guests, and the staff—and Blackstone—applaud.

This story ends here. But if you would like to try again, and perhaps solve the mystery of the long-ago Gentleman Jack, you can start over.

BLACKSTONE SHARES HIS MAGIC

Gentleman Jack's Magic Ball Trick

Take an ordinary ball.

In one hand take hold of a special rope, which has a piece of fine thread tied at each end. From only a short distance away, the thread cannot be seen.

Now, hold the string and the rope slightly apart.

Then make a track for the ball to run along.

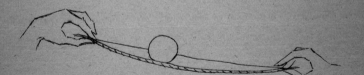

BLACKSTONE'S MAGIC ADVENTURES!

Use your wits and Blackstone's tricks to save the day!

☐ 56251-8 BLACKSTONE'S MAGIC ADVENTURE #1:
THE CASE OF THE MUMMY'S TOMB $1.95
☐ 56252-6   Canada $2.50

☐ 56253-4 BLACKSTONE'S MAGIC ADVENTURE #2
THE CASE OF THE GENTLEMAN GHOST $1.95
☐ 56254-2   Canada $2.50

☐ 56255-0 BLACKSTONE'S MAGIC ADVENTURE #3
THE CASE OF THE PHANTOM TREASURE $1.95
☐ 56256-9   Canada $2.50

Buy them at your local bookstore or use this handy coupon:
Clip and mail this page with your order

TOR BOOKS—Reader Service Dept.
P.O. Box 690, Rockville Centre, N.Y. 11571

Please send me the book(s) I have checked above. I am enclosing
$_____ (please add $1.00 to cover postage and handling).
Send check or money order only—no cash or C.O.D.'s.

Mr./Mrs./Miss _____
Address _____
City _____ State/Zip _____
Please allow six weeks for delivery. Prices subject to change without notice.

In the YOUR *AMAZING* adventures™ series, each book contains a new quest, new obstacles to be overcome, new mazes, and new dangers. And don't forget, *you* are the hero or heroine.

Now in print:

ZORK
A WHAT-DO-I-DO-NOW BOOK

☐ 57975-5 ZORK #1: THE FORCES OF KRILL $1.95
   57976-3 Canada $2.50

☐ 57980-1 ZORK #2: THE MALIFESTRO QUEST $1.95
   57981-X Canada $2.50

☐ 57985-2 ZORK #3: THE CAVERN OF DOOM $1.95
   57986-0 Canada $2.50

☐ 55989-4 ZORK #4: CONQUEST AT QUENDOR $1.95
   55990-8 Canada $2.50

Buy them at your local bookstore or use this handy coupon:
Clip and mail this page with your order

TOR BOOKS—Reader Service Dept.
P.O. Box 690, Rockville Centre, N.Y. 11571

**Please send me the book(s) I have checked above. I am enclosing
$_____ (please add $1.00 to cover postage and handling).
Send check or money order only—no cash or C.O.D.'s.**

Mr./Mrs./Miss _____
Address _____
City _____ State/Zip _____
**Please allow six weeks for delivery. Prices subject to change without
notice.**